For my mother who believed in me and taught me to believe in myself.

ISBN: 978-1-0881-0183-4

Library of Congress Control Number: 2023904670

Edited by Tamara Rittershaus
www.PictureBookTamara.com

Illustrations and Design by Santhya Shenbagam R.

Sweetwater Stories

Trixie
Learns to Trust

Cindy Roberts

Trixie yawned, stretched, and peeked out of her house inside the big tree on the edge of the woods. It was midafternoon, and usually she would still be sleeping, but she was hungry.

"I really shouldn't go out right now," she said to herself. "It's not safe."

She just had to go and find something to eat though, even if it meant she might be seen.

"I'll just go out for a quick bite," she thought to herself.

Normally, the family that lives in the house near her tree was not home at this time of day.

Trixie slowly crawled out.
"Yay! Nobody's here!"
She reached for the juicy blackberries
that were growing near the fence.

Suddenly, Trixie froze.

The lady from the house! In the yard!
"Oh no! What's she doing out here?"

Trixie ran back to the safety of
her tree and climbed high up into
the branches.

The lady who lives in the house
stood at the base of the tree
talking to Trixie.

"It's okay to come down. No one is
going to hurt you,"
but Trixie curled her tail around her
face and hid.

Over the next few days the lady looked for Trixie but Trixie stayed curled up and hidden in the branches of the tall tree.

Trixie remembered what her mother used to tell her. "People can be mean to raccoons. They don't like us to come around so we have to stay hidden."

The lady brought out some fruit and some cool water for Trixie.

"I can do this," Trixie said to herself. After the lady walked back to the porch, Trixie climbed slowly out of the tree.

She ate the fruit and drank the cool water that the lady had left out. "I'm so glad you came down to eat with me," the lady said. Trixie and the lady met outside for lunch every day.

Then one day, Trixie didn't come to eat. "Trixie, I hope you are okay," said the lady.

The next day the food was gone! "Did you come by when I wasn't looking?" the lady asked out loud. She took fruit and nuts out every day and waited, but she didn't see her raccoon friend.

"Purr purr purr." "What's that sound? Where's it coming from?" The lady leaned over the railing.
Trixie came out from under the porch. Two baby raccoons followed behind.

"Oh Trixie!" the lady exclaimed. "Your babies are so cute!"

"Who's that lady, Mama?" said Daisy, Trixie's daughter.

"We've never seen her before!" said Scooter, Trixie's son, in a scared voice.

"It's okay," said Trixie.

"She's the lady who lives in the house. Sometimes she leaves a snack for us."

Every day Trixie, Scooter, and Daisy came for lunch.

The lady who lives in the house sat and watched them
eat and play until nighttime.

And every night Trixie said, "Alright, Scooter and Daisy. It's getting late. It's time to go to bed."

"Ah Mama, can't we stay and play a little longer?"
Scooter asked.

"Yes! PLEASEEEE!" Daisy begged.

"No. Now say goodnight to the lady who lives in the house."

Trixie, Scooter, and Daisy all raised their front paws to wave to the lady.

"Goodnight to you too!" the lady who lives in the house said.

Trixie took Scooter and Daisy home and tucked them safely into their beds in their house in the hole in the big tree on the edge of the woods.

And every night, everyone, including the lady who lives in the house, went to sleep with a happy heart and a big smile on their faces.

Raccoon Facts

🐾 Raccoons are wild animals. Don't try to pet them. Watch them from a distance.

🐾 Raccoons are nocturnal animals but they do come out during the day sometimes to look for food.

🐾 Raccoons are known as opportunistic feeders. They eat what they can find in the wild and where humans live. Don't feed them. They can become a nuisance.

🐾 Raccoon babies are called kits. Mama raccoons have 2-5 babies per litter. They are normally born in early Spring.

🐾 A group of raccoons is called a gaze.

Ingram Content Group UK Ltd.
Milton Keynes UK
UKHW051136260523
422353UK00003B/28

9 781088 101834